3.7

Private Lily

Also by Sally Warner

Dog Years

Some Friend

Ellie and the Bunheads

Sort of Forever

Other books about Lily

Sweet & Sour Lily

Private Lily

by Sally Warner

illustrated by
Jacqueline Rogers

ALFRED A. KNOPF
New York

For Nancy Russell

THIS IS A BORZOI BOOK PUBLISHED BY ALFRED A. KNOPF, INC.

Text copyright © 1998 by Sally Warner.
Illustration copyright © 1998 by Jacqueline Rogers.
All rights reserved under International and Pan-American Copyright
Conventions. Published in the United States of America by Alfred A.
Knopf, Inc., New York, and simultaneously in Canada by Random House
of Canada Limited, Toronto. Distributed by Random House, Inc., New York.

Library of Congress Cataloging-in-Publication Data
Warner, Sally
Private Lily / by Sally Warner ;
illustrated by Jacqueline Rogers
p. cm.
Summary: After a series of unsuccessful attempts, six-year-old Lily suc-
ceeds in making a private space for herself in her small apartment.
ISBN 0-679-89137-4 (trade)
ISBN 0-679-99137-9 (lib. bdg.)
[1. Privacy, Right of—Fiction. 2. Family life—Fiction.]
I. Rogers, Jacqueline, ill. II. Title
PZ7.W24644Pr 1998
[Fic]—dc21   97-52932

www.randomhouse.com/kids/

Printed in the United States of America

10 9 8 7 6 5 4 3 2 1

CONTENTS

CHAPTER ONE
No Fair!

"It's not fair!" I yell at Case.

"It is too," Case says. "I'm older." My brother Casey is twelve, and I'm only six, but so what? I'm just as real as he is. How come he's the only one with his own room? He is sitting on his bed in his own private room right now, the big show-off.

I try to think of a way to win this fight. "Well, we should *share*," I say. "One night you get to sleep there, and the next night it's my turn."

"No way," Case says, and he starts reading his book again. Right in front of my face, like I've finished talking!

But I haven't finished. "We'll ask Mommy," I say.

My mommy is down in the basement doing laundry. I hate this stupid Philadelphia apartment we moved to last summer. At our old New Jersey house, the washing machine and dryer were right next to the kitchen. Everything was perfect then. I had my own room, for one thing.

When we moved, Mommy said that I was going to be her new roommate. Our two beds would fit in that room together.

And at first I thought, *Oh, boy!* I wouldn't have to sneak into my mommy's room at night for a snuggle. I could just hop from my bed onto her bed, *boi-oi-oi-ng!* She'd be right there, all the time. And I could play with all her stuff, too.

2

But now that's the trouble—she's right there, all the time. And none of her stuff is fun to play with, not really.

"Go ahead and ask her," Case says. He's not the tiniest bit worried. "Anyway," he says, looking around, "it's not like this is even a real room. It's just a bed with a curtain in front of it."

I want to grab that book right out of his hands and throw it across the room! "If you hate it so much, then give it to me," I say.

"I never said I hated it. But I think I need some privacy now," he says. He yawns to show me how bored he is, then pulls the striped curtain in front of his bed shut, with him behind it.

"Oh, yeah?" I shout. "Well, I need

privacy, too!" And I run into the bath-room and slam the door behind me.

He doesn't care. He doesn't even knock on the bathroom door and ask if I'm all right, which I am *not.*

I'm mad.

Like I told Case, it's no fair! I add this unfair thing to a whole list of things that are not fair. Here are some of the other things on the list, besides number one— he gets a room and I don't:

2. The TV picture is so bad in this apartment that you have to hold on to the antennas like they were magic wands to see anything, only then you can't see anything, because you are standing behind the TV set.

3. Mommy has a job now, and dinner is never ready when I want it to be.

4. And my daddy isn't here, because a mean judge said he had to go to jail. For taking stuff that wasn't his. But that's a secret, so *shhh.*

5. I can never find any of my toys, because most of the good stuff is still packed in boxes down in the apartment basement.

Except it isn't really an apartment, not like a tall, fancy building. Just one other person lives here, and his name is Buddy Haynes. He lives downstairs, and he owns this whole place.

The worst part about Buddy is that he

6

has to sit in a wheelchair all the time. The best part about Buddy is that he has a dog! That's another thing that's no fair:

6. We don't have a dog.

That's six bad things, and I'm six. But all of those terrible things would seem okay if only I had a place to go that was just for me. No one could come in without asking my permission, and even then I would probably say no.

I mash my ear against the bathroom door to hear if Mommy is back yet from the basement. Nope, not yet. Poor her! It's dark and spooky down there. I know, because sometimes I help her do the laundry.

There is only one tiny window in the basement, way up high, and one lightbulb on the ceiling. When you pull the wet clothes out of the washing machine, they hold on to each other like a bunch of big old spiders. It gives me the creeps. Not to mention what happens if you drop something on the floor, which is always dusty. Ick!

In fact, the only good part about helping Mommy with the laundry is getting to play with the dryer lint. I'm in charge of that, and I've already saved up a great big pile of it in an empty box. There's enough lint for a dog to sleep on, if he wanted to. Well, if it was a *little* dog.

Hey, even a pretend dog could have his own private place in this stupid building, and his own special lint bed, too! I'm the only person who has to share.

I'm the only extra person.

But when I look around the bathroom, I see something that is the answer to all my problems!

CHAPTER TWO
The Bathtub

"But how come I can't sleep in the bath-tub tonight?" I ask Mommy for the third time. The first two times I asked, she said *no,* which was not the right answer, so I am asking again.

My mommy sighs. "Lily, it's still wet from your bath."

"You could dry it out," I say, "then I could pile it up with pillows and stuff and make a cozy nest." I try to look cute, like a little squirrel or something.

"With what pillows?" Mommy asks me. "We don't have that many pillows," she says.

"Well, I've got one, and you have one, and Case has one. That makes three pillows," I say.

"She's not getting *my* pillow," Case calls out from behind his curtain. He is eating a bowl of strawberry ice cream in his own private room like he is the king of everything.

"You won't even share your *pillow* with me?" I ask him.

Mommy is talking again. She hates it when we fight, especially lately. "This has nothing to do with your brother, Lily. *I'm* telling you that it just won't work, that's all."

"Yeah," Case says. "What if you jam your toe up in the faucet during the night, like you did that one time? It got stuck, remember?"

I frown at him to shut him up. "I was just trying to make the water spray," I tell him. "That could have happened to anyone."

"Oh, you made the water spray, all right," Mommy says, shaking her head. "It took me half an hour to mop it all up."

"Thanks a lot, Case," I say to my brother, my voice growly.

"But that's another thing," my mommy is saying. "The faucet in the bathtub leaks a little bit, and you can't sleep in a leaky bed."

"She could always wear diapers," Case teases.

"Shut up, shut up!" I say. "Diapers are for babies!"

"And diapers only take care of leaks

that come from the inside, not the out-side," Mommy says. She is smiling now, even though I told Case to shut up. My mommy usually doesn't like bad language.

"Well, at least let me try sleeping in the bathtub," I say. "For just one night! *Please?*"

"Hmm," Mommy says. "I suppose I could hook one of our plastic buckets over the faucet to catch any drips. And we could put the cushions from the living room chair in the tub to make it soft-er. For just one night."

Case is shaking his head like he can't believe his ears. "You're going to let her do it?" he screeches. "This is the goofiest thing I ever heard!"

"Mind your own beeswax," I tell him. "This is between Mommy and me."

"But—but what if I have to use the bathroom when she's in there?" Case asks Mommy like I'm not even sitting here. His ears are turning red now, which only happens when he is really, really mad. This is so cool! I like Case most of the time, but not when he gets to have everything his own way.

"I'm sure that if you knock, Lily will tell you to come in," Mommy says. "She can always pull the shower curtain shut to give you some privacy."

"I'm sure she *won't* let me in," Case says. He is exactly right about that! "And anyway," he says, "who wants to, um, go to the bathroom with her lying right there?"

"Well, Lily?" Mommy says, turning to me. "Don't you think Casey has a point?"

"It's only for one night," I say in my sweetest voice. "And Case can use our *other* bucket."

"I'm not using *any* bucket if I have to go to the bathroom," Case yells.

"Go *now*, then," I say, and I walk over to the big, squashy living room chair we always sit in whenever we use the telephone. I pick up one of the blue and green flowered cushions and give a big pretend yawn. "I'm getting sleepy," I say.

"You faker!" Case says in a loud voice.

I yawn again, for real this time.

"You'd better do as she says," Mommy tells my brother. "And brush your teeth

while you're at it, Case. I'll go get Lily's bedding, and the bucket. The *two* buckets."

"This is nuts," Case says in his most muttery voice. But he stomps into the bathroom and slams the door.

After he's finished in there, and after my mommy washes her face and brushes her teeth, the bathroom will be all mine—my own private little room.

For one night, anyway!

CHAPTER THREE
Why Not?

I am the sorest I have ever been in my whole life so far.

Last night started out great. Mommy put a night-light in the bathroom, in case I woke up and forgot I was sleeping in the bathtub. The only trouble with that idea was that I never fell asleep in the bathtub, so how could I wake up?

Here is what went wrong:

1. I could still feel the bottom of the tub, even underneath all those cushions. It felt like I was sleeping on the sidewalk.

2. I bonked my elbow on the

side of the tub, and it hurt like crazy. I yelled for Mommy, and she petted me until I felt better. She said I had hit my funny bone, but *ha-ha,* very funny. That is not my idea of a very good joke.

3. The toilet looked scary at night, like a big guy sitting there with no head on him. Even with the night-light on.

4. And on top of everything else, I knocked the bucket off the faucet. All of those drips added up to make one big sploosh, and it fell right on my feet.

So I ended up crawling into Mommy's bed—because it was the middle of the night and all of my covers were in the bathtub, wet. She groaned but lifted up the covers like she had been waiting for me the whole time.

Now it is morning, and when Case went into the bathroom, he saw the wet cushions and thought I had a little accident during the night. He didn't say anything, but I *know* that's what he thought. It's none of his beeswax if I have a little accident sometimes, but this time I didn't! So no fair.

But at breakfast, when I try to explain to him about the bucket, he just smiles and opens his eyes wide like he doesn't believe me. "Case, shut up!" I tell him.

"I didn't say anything," he says, and he carries his cereal bowl to the sink like Mr. Perfect.

My mommy bangs down her coffee cup. "Lily, I want you to be a little more careful about your language," she says. "You can't keep telling everyone in the world to shut up. It's vulgar and rude."

"I don't tell everyone that," I say. "Just Case. Because of his big fat mouth."

"Lily!" Mommy says. She's *really* mad now.

"I didn't say a *word*," Case says. But when Mommy isn't looking, he grins at me. Then he turns around to look at his behind, like he's afraid he wet his pants or something.

"Shut up! Quit teasing!" I yell again, and I run into the bathroom and slam the door before Mommy can scold me again.

The bathroom looks more normal

during the daytime, I am glad to see. The toilet is not scary anymore. It's just a toilet again.

Case always leaves for school before Mommy and I leave. After I hear the front door shut, I come out of the bathroom like nothing is wrong. Mommy hands me my lunch, I put on my sweater and pick up my backpack, and we go out the door.

I am in the first grade at Betsy Ross Primary School. I liked my old school better, before we moved, but Betsy Ross isn't so bad. And maybe I am just remembering the good old days when I was in kindergarten! It's possible.

My teacher's name is Ms. Marshall. She wears her hair in a ponytail, just like a kid. When she gets frazzled, her hair starts to hang in her face. This usually doesn't happen until lunch, but sometimes it happens in the morning, at nutrition break. She is very pretty, even when her face turns pink and she has to do her yoga breathing.

It seems like there are about a hundred kids in my class, but I am starting to be friends with two of them. Their names are Daisy Greenough and LaVon Hamilton. They were already friends with each other, but they are making room for me.

Mommy walks me to school every day, and then she keeps walking until she gets to the bookstore where she works. The best part about walking to school with my mommy is that we get to talk alone, without Case. I have something I want to tell her today. "I have an idea," I say. We step over some broken glass on the sidewalk.

"Uh-oh," she says, like it is a joke.

"No, this is for real," I tell her. "It's a *good* idea."

"Okay, let's hear it," Mommy says.

"My idea is that we move again, but this time we get a bigger apartment!" I say. "One where everybody gets their own room." I can't believe she has never thought of this before.

"So how big an apartment would that be, do you think?" Mommy asks me.

I get a little bit nervous, because this sounds like a trick question. But maybe it's not. "Well, we need to have three bedrooms," I say.

"Three bedrooms," Mommy says back just like an echo. "Anything else?"

I walk around a bulgy, smelly pile of garbage bags that look like they are growing out of the sidewalk, and I think. "There should be room for our own washing machine," I say.

"Anything else?" Mommy says again.

"We should have another bathroom!" I say. "Or maybe two more bathrooms. That way no one would ever have to wait."

"Three bedrooms and three bathrooms," Mommy says, and she shakes her head sadly. "I'm sorry, sweetie, but it's not going to happen. Not any time soon, anyway."

"But why not?" I say. I can't believe

she's saying no to my great idea so fast!
"Okay," I say, "just two bathrooms, then.
But we could do it. I know it's a lot of
work to move, but Casey and I would
help you pack!"

"Lily, it's not that," Mommy says. "It's
the money."

"What money?" I ask.

Mommy laughs. "That's just the problem, honey—what money?"

I frown. "I don't get it," I say. I hate it
when I don't get jokes.

"It's like this," Mommy says. "When you
rent an apartment, you pay money for it
every month. You don't own it. And the
owner figures out how much to charge
based on how big the apartment is, and
so on."

"I *still* don't get it," I say. "And anyway, how come we had to move?" When we lived in New Jersey it was in our own house. We didn't have to pay any stupid rent.

"Lily, I thought I explained all that," Mommy says. "Without your father around, I couldn't afford to keep our house—or the car, for that matter. We needed to start over, baby. I just figured it would be easier to do that in the city. I could get a job, and we could walk or take the bus when we needed to go someplace."

"Yeah, but now we don't have enough room to even live in," I say. Can't she see that?

Now Mommy sighs. "Lily," she says,

"when I am making more money, maybe we can move to a bigger place. But it will be a while before that happens."

We are almost at school. I am sore and tired and mad, and now I feel like crying. I bet I am the only kid in the whole first grade who had to sleep in the bathtub last night!

"I know you want your own room, sweetie," my mommy is saying.

"Yeah, I do," I tell her. "I need some privacy." That's what Case always says. Well, he's not the only one!

"We all do," Mommy says. She reaches out to straighten my sweater, and I jump back like she is a big bee with a stinger.

A hurt look pops onto her face and

she puts her hand away. "Have a good day at school, darling," she says.

I don't answer her. I don't hug her good-bye, either. Instead, I stomp up the steps that lead to the school's front door. I don't look back.

I don't like making my mommy sad, but sometimes I can't help it!

And anyway, she makes me sad, too.

CHAPTER FOUR
Sharing

Daisy is in the cloakroom hanging up her zebra-striped backpack. She has yellow hair. Some daisies are yellow, or at least their belly buttons are, so that's how you remember her name. I wish *I* had yellow hair.

My hair is brown, and I have freckles on my face. Just what I need.

"Hi, Lily," Daisy says. "It's late! I thought maybe you were going to be absent."

"Nope, I'm present," I say, and I hang up my stinky backpack, which used to be Case's. Lucky me!

"You look funny, though," Daisy says.

"I slept in the bathtub last night, that's all," I tell her.

Daisy's eyes are big and round. "You *did?*" she asks, her voice getting all squeaky.

In the classroom Ms. Marshall is clapping her hands. This means it is time for everyone to take their seats. She says she has to save her voice for the important stuff.

Daisy and I go and sit down. She gets to sit next to LaVon, who turns around and waves at me. I have to sit next to Marcus, who is always getting into trouble.

First we do numbers. As usual, I have trouble with my eights. My snaky line never ends up meeting at the top where it should. I can do a perfect eight if I put a little circle on top of another one, like a snowman. But *oh no,* Ms. Marshall wants us to draw an eight with just one line.

For some reason Marcus can do his eights perfectly, even though he can't stand in line without poking the kid in front of him—who is usually me. It's no fair!

Ms. Marshall sneaks up behind me and makes me jump. "Close them up at the top," she whispers, tapping her fingernail on my worksheet. "Don't let anything fall into your eights, Lily," she says with a smile.

I imagine a big mob of cooties trying to jump into the open top of the eight I am drawing, and I press down hard on my pencil and finally close it up. But *pop!* The point of my pencil breaks and bounces into nowhere. I raise my hand to go sharpen my pencil, but Ms. Marshall doesn't see me.

Oh, great, I think. *Now I will never finish this stupid worksheet.*

But before I can worry too much, it is time for nutrition break.

This is really the same as snack time, but at Betsy Ross Primary School everything has an important name. The sun is shining this morning, so we get to go outside.

But first we all crowd into the cloakroom and start feeling inside our bags for something good to eat. I pull out an apple and some string cheese.

LaVon's backpack is shaped like a

bear. It even has a fuzzy tail! She peeks inside the bear, sticks in her hand, and pulls out some peanut butter and jelly crackers, her favorite.

Daisy sighs and reaches into her striped backpack. She pulls out a sack of knobbly little muffins. Seeds and nuts are sticking out of them like crazy. Daisy's mom cooks all the stuff they eat, and she doesn't believe in sugar. LaVon and I feel so sorry for Daisy! That's why we are always sharing our goodies with her.

Daisy tries to share with us, too. Sometimes the food she brings from home tastes good, but sometimes it is just plain strange. Today is one of those days. "Want some string cheese?" I say to her as we walk outside.

She nods, and her yellow bangs bounce on her forehead. "Want a peanut butter and jelly cracker?" LaVon asks too, trying to be nice like me. You can tell LaVon wishes she could eat up all her own crackers, but Daisy is our friend. We can't let her starve.

"Yeah, thanks," Daisy says, taking one. "Do you guys want a muffin?"

"No thank you," LaVon and I say politely. LaVon shakes her head *no* so fast that all three braids whip back and forth. She has one on each side and one in the back. And she has the cutest barrettes you ever saw. They always match her clothes perfectly. Today they are bright yellow, like jellybeans.

Nothing I wear ever matches perfectly. No fair.

"Hey," I say when we are on the climbing structure, "do you guys have your own bedroom at home?" I try to take a bite of my apple, but it is hard when practically all of your teeth have fallen out. Your front ones, anyway. So far I am not getting very much nutrition.

"I don't have my own room. I share with my big sister," LaVon says. "It's really fun! She tells me stories and stuff. And she braids my hair and lets me listen to her music."

"Huh," I say. I don't think Case would ever do that. He tries to pretend that I'm invisible most of the time. I turn to Daisy. "What about you?" I ask. "Do you have your own room?"

She is chewing on one of those prickly

muffins. She swallows hard, like a pinecone is stuck in her throat. "Uh-huh," she croaks, nodding yes.

"You're lucky," I say, my voice all gloomy. "I have to share."

"With your *brother?*" LaVon asks me. She makes a face—not the funny kind.

"No, with my mommy," I say. "But it's just for a little while," I add quickly. "Only until we move to a bigger apartment."

"Do you sleep in the same *bed?*" LaVon asks. She is looking at me like I am a different person all of a sudden. A weirdo.

But I'm *not* a weirdo! Oh, why did I say anything about bedrooms in the first place? Next they're going to ask about my daddy. And that's none of their

beeswax, even if they are my new best friends.

"We don't sleep in the same bed," I say, like that's the stupidest thing I ever heard. "Just in the same room. And it's a big room. *Real* big. I almost can't even see her, it's so big."

LaVon licks her fingertip and uses it to brush the crumbs from her face, like a kitten. She doesn't say anything more, which makes me feel bad.

Daisy brushes seeds and nuts from her sweater. "Well, I think that sounds like fun," she says, sounding all fakey. "I get lonely in my room at night all by myself. Especially when it's dark." She is acting like she is sorry for me. That makes me feel even worse than being a weirdo.

"Well, *duh*," I say. "It's always dark at night, Daisy."

Daisy's eyes get round again, and she opens her mouth to say something. She looks just like this old doll I used to have! But before any words come out of her mouth, Ms. Marshall is clapping her hands to line everybody up. That means it's time to go back to class.

And another fun nutrition break is over. Whoopee. My stomach makes a growling noise you can hear a mile away.

So here is a list of the people I am mad at:

1. Case, for just about saying I wet the bed.

2. Mommy, for not moving us to a big-enough apartment.

3. LaVon, for always matching. And for having a sister and not a brother. And for thinking I am a weirdo.

4. Daisy, for feeling sorry for me.

I am so tired that I think I could curl up and sleep for two whole days.

Even in a bathtub.

CHAPTER FIVE

The Kitchen Table

"I've got another idea about having my own private place," I say at dinner. "A *better* idea."

Case swallows his bite of hamburger. "Wow," he says, "even better than sleeping in the bathtub?"

"Shut up," I say without even thinking.

"Don't talk like that, Lily," Mommy says, spreading mustard on her hamburger bun. Ick.

I stick my fork into a Tater Tot and drag it through some ketchup. I make a perfect eight on my plate with the ketchup. Where is Ms. Marshall when you really need her?

"Don't play with your food, sweetie-pie," my mommy tells me. "Let's hear your new idea," she says.

"Yeah, let's hear it," Case says, like an echo.

I take a deep breath. "Okay, well, I'll tell you," I say to Mommy. "My idea is that I make a little cave under the kitchen table. Just for one night."

"*This* kitchen table?" my mommy asks, looking confused.

"Mom, this is the only kitchen table we have," Case says. He thinks he's so smart! "Please pass the Tater Tots."

Mommy hands him the bowl, then turns to look at me. "Lily, do you mean that you want to sleep on the floor?"

"On the floor under the *table*," I explain to her. "See, we could put my bedspread over the top of the table! After we wash the dishes, I mean. That would turn it into a cave underneath."

"But you'd still be sleeping on the floor," Mommy says. "I can't have you sleeping on the floor, honey."

Case grins. "Maybe she could use those chair cushions again," he says. "If they're *dry* yet, I mean."

"Shut up," I say. I tear off a piece of hamburger bun. I just wish we had a parrot I could feed it to. I would trade Case for a parrot any day. Hey, and then I could have his hidey-hole! A parrot *and* my own private place. Cool.

"Lily," Mommy says. But I can tell she is thinking. "Well, I suppose we could try it—for just one night."

"Mom, I was kidding about her using the cushions again!" Case says. A Tater Tot almost drops out of his mouth, he is so surprised.

"Yes, but it's not a bad idea," Mommy says.

"It is too! It's a *terrible* idea!" Case almost yells. "I don't want her sleeping in the same room as me."

"I'll be in my own room," I say. "My own little cave room under the table."

"Oh, it will be little, all right," Mommy says. "Come on, Case, it won't be so bad. At least you'll have peace and quiet if you need to use the bathroom tonight."

Case slams down his fork. "I'm not going to have any peace and quiet with Lily in the same room as me, Mom. She'll keep yapping at me all night long!"

"I don't yap," I tell him. "And anyway, once you pull your curtain shut and I'm inside my cave, it will be like there's a wall down the middle of the room."

"Do you promise?" Case asks me, a scowl on his face.

"I promise. Just don't you bother *me*, that's all," I tell him.

"Nobody's going to be bothering any-one," my mommy says. She always likes to look on the bright side, even when there isn't one.

Case gives a big sigh, like he's the unluckiest person in the whole wide world to have a little sister like me. "Well, okay," he says. "I guess we can give it a try—for just one night."

"Mommy already said yes," I tell him.

"But thanks for cooperating, honey," Mommy says to him, and she gives him a big smile. "I'm sure it will work out fine," she says. "Anyway, how bad could it be?"

CHAPTER SIX
Weirdos

I'll tell you how bad it could be—*real* bad. Terrible.

First, the bedspread didn't reach all the way to the floor, so it wasn't really like a cave room in there at all. It was like sleeping under somebody's bed.

I could see the bottom part of our kitchen if I turned one way, and the bottom part of the living room if I turned the other way. And if I looked up, I saw the bottom of the kitchen table. Big wow.

Here is what else went wrong:

2. One of the chair cushions

was still a little bit wet from last night, and it smelled funny.

3. Case kept reading or drawing after I went to bed, and his light bothered me.

4. But when he turned his light off, the dark bothered me even more!

And here is the worst thing of all!

5. Just when I was finally falling asleep, a spider ran across my face! At least I think it was a spider. It sure had a lot of legs. I screeched, and I jumped up so fast that I bonked my head on the bottom of the table. Ow! Case's light went back on.

That was something that turned out

all right, anyway. Case was pretty nice to me after the part about the spider. He got me a glass of cool water and patted my shoulder in a *there,there* way. Then he brought me some Kleenexes so I could blow my nose.

It looked a little like I was crying, but I wasn't.

Then Case went on a spider hunt while I stood on the living room chair. It didn't have any cushions on it, so the chair felt all lumpy and bumpy under my feet.

I am not really afraid of spiders, by the way. Only when they go for a hike across my face in the middle of the night, that's all.

Case finally said, "Hah! Gotcha," to a

speck on the floor. Then he picked up the speck in a clean Kleenex, opened the window, and dropped everything outside. I didn't even call him a litterbug, but I will pick up the Kleenex in the morning—if it is still on the sidewalk. And if there is no spider hiding inside.

There was still a lot of night left, so I crawled in bed with my mommy again. Just like before, she groaned. I guess she had been expecting me. She was too tired to go get my covers from under the table and make my bed, I guess, so she let me stay.

Now it is morning again. My covers have been put away, and the blue and green cushions are back on the big squashy chair. We are eating breakfast, but everyone is quiet this morning. Even me.

I can still feel those spider feet.

I wish I didn't have to go to school today! I feel funny about seeing Daisy and LaVon again. Are we still friends?

I started out just wanting my own bedroom, or at least my own private place. I didn't even think about Daisy's room or LaVon's room. Not at first, not until I started yapping to them about it. And I didn't think about how strange it is that Mommy is my roommate.

But now my two best friends know about my weirdo family. At least they know some things about it. They probably won't want to play with me anymore.

I cough a little bit and try to look sick.

"Cover your mouth when you do that, Lily," Mommy says. "And get your back-pack."

So much for being sick, I think. Nobody around here cares about me!

I get to school a little early, so I have already taken my seat when Daisy and LaVon come into the classroom. I pretend that I am very busy looking at my desk.

LaVon touches my back on the way to her desk. I jump about a mile. "Hi," she says, smiling big. Today her barrettes are lime green. They look like you could crunch them up like candy.

"Hi," I say. I am surprised any sound comes out of my frozen mouth. Hey, maybe LaVon has forgotten all about yesterday!

LaVon leans over and whispers in my ear. "I brought some extra peanut butter and jelly crackers today," she says. "For you-know-who."

You-know-who, I think, confused. Who? Oh, LaVon must mean that she brought them for Daisy! Daisy, with her weirdo snacks.

Wait, I think all of a sudden, *maybe I am not the only kid in the first grade with something goofy about her family.*

Now Daisy herself walks up to me. Her yellow hair shines in the morning sun. I wish I was as pretty as Daisy! "Hi," she says.

Ms. Marshall is clapping her hands for everyone to take their seats.

"I brought some stickers for you and

LaVon," Daisy says in a hurry. "Sparkly ones! I'll give them to you guys at nutrition break."

"Thanks," I say.

Marcus is listening in. "Ooooh," he teases, "stickers! For *me?*" He rubs his hands together and blinks his eyes real fast like a cartoon lady who has just gotten a box of chocolates.

"No, *not* for you," Daisy says, and she makes a face at him.

"Anyway, mind your own beeswax," I tell him. I am feeling brave. Daisy and I look at each other and giggle.

But I am thinking, *stickers!* They are one of my two favorite things in the world. Here is my other favorite thing:

2. Rubber stamps.

Then I frown for just a second. Hey, is Daisy giving me stickers just because she feels sorry for me? But then I smile again. No, she's giving them to LaVon, too. And Daisy doesn't feel sorry for LaVon. They have been friends since before kindergarten. Anyway, nobody could feel sorry for LaVon.

"Lily?" Ms. Marshall is saying. "Would you like to pass out these worksheets for me?"

Yes-s-s-s! I jump up so fast that Marcus pretends I have knocked him off his chair. Everybody laughs.

But I don't even care, because Ms. Marshall has finally called on me to be her helper. And Daisy and LaVon are still my friends. This is great, because I do *not* want to have privacy when I am at school. Just at home.

Also, I am happy that I am not the only weirdo at Betsy Ross.

In fact, I am thinking, this place is probably *packed* with weirdos!

CHAPTER SEVEN
The Closet

There is still the great big problem about no privacy for me in our weensy apartment, but I have one last idea. It's a really good one, too. "Hey, Mommy?" I say after dinner.

"Oh, no, here we go again," Case says. He runs over to the big telephone chair and flings himself down on the cushions like an octopus, so I can't take them. And he was my friend last night!

I pretend that my brother is invisible and I cannot hear his yapping. "You know what, *Mommy?*" I say, looking only at her.

"What, sweetie-pie?" my mommy says.

She is still in the good dinnertime mood that lasts until you have to start cleaning up.

"Well, you know your closet?" I say.

From the comfortable chair Case laughs. "Of course she knows her closet. Its name is Fred!" he says. He is acting very silly tonight, I think. Worse than a little kid.

I still pretend that I can't hear his yapping, but this is getting harder to do.

"What *about* my closet, Lily?" Mommy says. Now one wrinkly little line is on her forehead, just like someone drew it there with a crayon. "Did you spill something in my closet?" she asks. She starts to get up from the table. Uh-oh, I think her good mood is almost over for tonight!

"No, no," I say in a hurry. "Nothing bad happened. It's just that I never noticed how big that closet is. It's huge, Mommy!"

"It doesn't seem all that big to me," my mommy says, but she sits back down again. "Everything is so jumbled in there that I can never find what I'm looking for half the time."

Here comes my great idea! "Well," I say, "that's because of all those shoe boxes and everything that are piled up on the floor."

"What are you saying?" Case asks me. "That Mom's closet would be perfect if it weren't for all the clothes in it?" He draws circles around his ears with his fingers like I am really goofy.

I don't tell my brother to shut up, but

I imagine a bunch of spiders scooting across *his* face at night. A whole parade of them! With a little brass band in front!

I give Mommy a big sweet smile to get her ready for my plan. "I'm not talking about the clothes," I tell her. "But if we moved all those boxes and everything that are on the floor, then there would be enough room."

"Enough room for what?" Mommy asks me. The wrinkly line on her forehead is back again.

"I know, I know!" Case says, raising his hand and waving it around like he is the only person in class with the right answer. "She wants to *sleep* in there!" he says, and then he laughs just like a hyena on a National Geographic special.

This is too much laughing and yapping for me, especially since he guessed right about my plan. "Shut up!" I tell him. "This is just between Mommy and me. And anyway, what's so strange about sleeping in Mommy's closet? It could be like my own little room."

"This is just pathetic," Case growls, mad all of a sudden, and he jumps off the chair and stomps into his hidey-hole. He yanks his red and white striped curtain shut, which means *Do Not Disturb*. No matter what.

"Who's he so mad at?" I ask Mommy. "At least Casey's got his own room. I'm the one who needs some privacy around here."

"You and me both," my mommy says.

Huh—and I thought she *liked* being roommates with me!

"Casey isn't mad at you, Lily," Mommy explains, "and he's not angry with me, either. I think he just wishes we could settle down in our new place, that's all. You know, he wants our lives to get back to normal."

"I almost can't remember normal anymore," I say. Now *I* am starting to get sad. "Were we normal when we lived in New Jersey, and I had my own bedroom?"

My mommy pulls me onto her lap. "No, honey. *This* is normal now," she says, and she gives me a hug. "Normal is when we are together," she says, "*wherever* we are."

I snuggle into her. "Yeah," I say, "but

sometimes we're together too close. It makes me feel all jangly inside. That's why I wanted my own private little place."

"Well," Mommy says, "we could try clearing the closet floor, I guess. But where would we put all my things?"

I am ready to answer this. "We could stack the boxes against the wall outside the closet," I say. "Very neatly!" I add.

"And then you could sleep on the floor," Mommy says, smiling. "On the big squashy cushions."

"I'd have my own door and everything," I say. Even Casey doesn't have his own door!

"But there's no window in my closet, Lily," Mommy warns me. "And no plug for a night-light, either. It'll be dark and stuffy."

"I don't care," I say bravely. "Let me try it!"

"For just one night?" Mommy asks me. She sounds a little bit teasing, but I don't care.

"Okay," I say, "for just one night. But if it works out, maybe I can move in there—for good."

Mommy just shakes her head and smiles at me.

But like I said, I don't even care. I know this plan is going to work out great!

CHAPTER EIGHT
The Stupid Prize

What a stupid idea this is.

In fact, maybe it is the stupidest idea in the whole wide world! I should get some kind of a prize. The *stupid* prize.

This plan isn't even starting out right. It takes a long time for Mommy to empty her closet floor, and she is in a very bad mood by the time she is done. And it's already bedtime, but we have to sweep out the closet and inspect it for spiders before we can put the chair cushions inside.

We search it one more time, just to make sure about the spiders.

Case doesn't say a word. He just stays behind his curtain.

Finally, *finally*, it is time for me to crawl under the covers in my mommy's closet. She is still reading in bed, so her light is on at first.

"Well, good night," I tell Mommy for the third time. "I'm going to bed now!" I am a little nervous about shutting the closet door with me inside. But I want to, because that is the whole point about having a door, isn't it?

"Nighty-night," Mommy says. She doesn't even look up from her book this time.

"I'm closing the door now," I say.

"Why don't you leave it open?" my mommy asks, looking up from her book. "That way you'll get some air."

"I don't need air, I need privacy," I tell her, and I pull the closet door shut. Most of the way, at least.

"Suit yourself," Mommy says from her comfortable bed.

So apart from not having any air to breathe, here is what is wrong with sleeping in Mommy's closet:

1. Everything.

It is so dark in here that I can't even see any shadows. A monster could be staring straight into my face, and I would not see it. That could be dangerous!

And whenever I sit up fast, which is very often, my head bumps into Mommy's clothes. It surprises me every single time, too, and surprises are not good in the middle of the night. Everybody knows that.

Doesn't anybody care?

I'm only six!

I push the door open a little bit wider. "Are you all right in there?" Mommy asks me. It has been dark in her room for a long time now. I thought she was asleep.

"I'm fine. I'm just breathing for a minute," I say.

I don't *feel* fine, but I don't want to tell my mommy that. And anyway, I am out of plans now, so this last one has to work! But my eyes are getting blinky, and my chin is starting to wobble.

Uh-oh, this is my secret sign that I am about to cry.

Instead I make a gaspy sound. "There, I'm finished breathing," I say, and I start to shut the door again.

"Lily, wait," Mommy's voice says in the dark.

"Okay," I say. I wait, but nothing happens.

"Aren't you feeling kind of lonely in the closet?" she finally asks.

"Yeah," I say, "but—but I don't think there's enough room for you in here, too. Sorry." A tear sneaks out of my eye and starts to creep down my face.

"Well, we could always put the covers back on your regular bed again," Mommy says.

I jump to my feet and bump into Mommy's clothes one last time. "Okay," I tell her. "If you insist."

"I do," Mommy says, yawning. "You go potty while I get everything ready."

When I walk into the little hall next to

the bathroom, Case's voice comes floating out of the living room. "What's the matter with sleeping in Mom's closet?" he asks. "Didn't it work?"

"It worked great," I tell him. "But Mommy thought I should move, that's all."

"Huh," Case says from behind his curtain.

I go to the bathroom and wash my hands. When I come back out, Case is standing there waiting for me. Oh, great.

"What's the matter?" I ask him. "Did you have a little *accident?*"

"No," he says, grinning, "but I do have a little plan. It might help give you some privacy! And then maybe we could all get some sleep around here."

"Huh," I say. I thought my own privacy plans were pretty good.

"You inspired me, Lily," Case says. "I never would have thought of my plan if it hadn't been for all the ideas you've come up with lately."

That's more like it, I think. "You have a plan?" I ask him. "For me? For real, Case?"

"What's going on out there?" Mommy's voice calls out. "It's the middle of the night!"

"Yeah, it's for real," Case whispers. "Now go to sleep, Lily-bug."

There isn't even such a thing as a lily-bug, but I don't care *what* he calls me.

Not if he has a plan.

Sometimes my big brother is pretty cool. And next to me, he has the best ideas in the whole wide world!

CHAPTER NINE
Lily's Private Place

At breakfast this morning, which is Saturday, Case tells Mommy about this store a few blocks away that sells used furniture. He is always talking about stuff like that, because he loves the olden days. In fact, Mommy calls Case her junk hound, like that's a good thing.

Case says he saw something in the window there that could give me some privacy! And so after breakfast we all walk over to the used-furniture store to take a look.

At first I am mad at Case. I don't see

anything good we can use. Is he trying to play a trick on me?

But Mommy smiles. "Look over there at the folding screen," she says.

I don't see a regular screen, not like the kind you put in your window to keep the flies out. But I do see something tall. It is made up of three long, skinny rectangles, sort of like picture frames. Hinges hold the three parts together. Strips of scraggly old cloth hang inside the frames.

Mommy says we could put new cloth there, and that would give me privacy. She says it would be a little bit like having a standing-up shower curtain.

I am having trouble picturing this.

Case says that people use folding screens to hide something ugly in a room.

Then he pokes me in the ribs and laughs. I poke him back. And even though the screen is kind of banged up and raggedy, my mommy buys it. I guess she knows what she's doing. One thing our family is good at is fixing up broken things!

We carry our folding screen home and take it down into the spooky basement. Case and Mommy say that we will make it look as good as new. Better than new!

First Mommy takes off all the rags from the screens' frames and throws them away. She says that we will replace the old cloth with new cloth later on.

Then Casey hammers in some nails that are popping out. *Blam, blam!* Then we all sandpaper away the peeling paint. I like using sandpaper.

But uh-oh, I think. Now my folding screen looks even worse than when we started. Case sees the look on my face. He says "Just wait," and my mommy asks me what color I wanted the screen to be.

So I say red, of course!

She says "Of course!" too, and then she laughs.

We all go to the paint store the very next minute and buy a little can of red paint and three brushes. We also buy some hoagies on the way home and sit on the front steps to eat them. But we are too busy to sit there very long!

We race upstairs to our apartment and put on our oldest clothes. Then we go back down to the basement. Casey puts the folding screen on top of a piece of cardboard, and we all start painting.

My mommy paints the top of the screen, Case paints the middle, and I paint the bottom part—because that's how tall we are.

We hardly get into any fights either. You should never start a fight when everyone is holding a paintbrush, by the way. I learned that lesson the last time Case and I painted something together.

Mommy says we could walk over to the cloth store while the paint is drying and asks if Case wants to come too. He says "No!" really loud. He says he is going to lie down and take a little nap.

But that is okay with me, because even though Casey helped with the plan, it is my screen! And my mommy says I get to choose whatever cloth I want for it.

As long as the cloth looks good with red, she says.

But that part is going to be easy, because everything looks good with red.

There are so many different cloths to choose from! First I walk up and down the aisles in the store, trying to see everything. Then I *run* up and down the aisles. What if I miss something really good?

I feel like my head is going to pop, there are so many patterns and colors.

Do I want the jungle-printed cloth? No, I'm not so sure I want to be staring at snakes and tigers right before I fall asleep.

Do I want the polka dots? No, they might look like eyeballs in the middle of the night.

Do I want the cloth that has Little Bo-Peep all over it, looking for her sheep? No way! She looks too pink and fluffy. Sometimes I am pink, but I am never fluffy.

Finally Mommy says that I have to make up my mind—*right now.* Before I can start running up and down the aisles again, though, she shows me two cloths I haven't seen before. One is white with little red hearts all over it. I like it! It makes me feel cheerful and sweet, which is the way I wish I was.

But the other cloth is frogs! Big frogs, little frogs, frogs sitting on lily pads, frogs hiding *under* lily pads.

Frogs and Lilys match perfectly. And frogs make me feel bouncy!

Frogs win.

And anyway, green looks good with red. Everybody knows that.

Mommy pays, and we walk home. I carry the bag and sniff my brand-new cloth every few steps. It smells so good!

We get home just in time, because it is starting to rain.

Case is getting up from his nap when we open the front door. He makes some popcorn, and we watch a funny movie together on TV while my mommy measures and sews the cloth.

We take turns holding the antennas.

I want to help sew, but Mommy says I *am* helping, just by watching TV.

Then Case brings my brand-new red folding screen up from the basement. The paint is all dry! Mommy attaches the frog cloth to the screen, and we all stand back to admire it.

I can't believe it, my privacy screen looks so good.

Casey says that nobody else in the whole wide world has a screen like mine.

We take it into the bedroom. I tell Mommy that maybe I want my bed pulled away from the wall a little bit, so we try that. We put the new screen next to my bed. It's like a green froggy wall!

Then Case moves my night table here and there, trying it in different places. The table ends up connecting my bed to the wall, like a little bridge. My desk and my little bookcase make another little bridge. And just like magic, there is a private place to play, right between my bed and the wall!

"Would you like to put a picture up on your wall?" Mommy asks me.

My wall! A picture! I think for a minute. "If Case will draw me one," I say. My brother is the best artist you ever saw.

"I guess I could draw you a cartoon," he says slowly.

"Yes-s-s-s!" I say. This is turning out to be a perfect day!

Case goes off to draw a cartoon for me.

My mommy smiles. "Well, I guess you have at least *some* privacy now, sweetie. A little bit, anyway. Lily's private place," she says, looking around.

"I've got a *lot* of privacy," I say. "If someone wants to come into my room, they'll have to say *'Knock, knock!'* Just like with Case."

"Knock, knock," Mommy says, practicing. It's good to practice.

"Is it bedtime yet?" I ask her. "Because I'm kind of tired," I say.

Mommy smiles. "No, it's not bedtime yet," she says. "But you might want to play in your room while I fix dinner."

Play in my room! Where nobody can see me! "Okay," I say, like it is no big deal. "I guess I'll figure out where to put my stuffed animals and dolls."

"Good luck," Mommy says, laughing now. "I'll call you when dinner is ready, sweetie."

"Yeah," I say. "And if I don't hear you, try knocking on one of the frogs. Okay?"

"Okay," she says.

When she goes, I sit down on my bed and look around my room. I have the most normal feeling in my heart since we moved.

And I am thinking, *Maybe Philadelphia isn't so bad!*

    1. It has Mommy and Case in it.

    2. And my friends at school are here.

    3. And so is my new private room.

I *love* my room. It's little, but it's all mine.

And not just for one night, either!